Oliver Guy Magee

A Summer Outing

A Farce-comedy in Three Acts

Oliver Guy Magee

A Summer Outing
A Farce-comedy in Three Acts

ISBN/EAN: 9783337054106

Printed in Europe, USA, Canada, Australia, Japan

Cover: Foto ©Andreas Hilbeck / pixelio.de

More available books at **www.hansebooks.com**

A Summer Outing.

A FARCE-COMEDY IN THREE ACTS,

By Oliver Guy Magee.

Oliver Guy Magee's

GAYEST AND HAPPIEST FARCE-COMEDY,

.. A ..

Summer

Outing.

THE REGISTER:

THE WONDER WORKER, Prof. Lectric Carr, an inventor and a hot tamale,..

THE WINGLESS ANGEL, Otto Sight, his cousin..............

THE MERRY HOST. Herrmann Pumpernickel,...................

THE LEARNED LAWYER, Fuller Tawk, his name an index to his character,...

THE BELL BOY, Hall Work, also elevator boy, with many ups and downs in life,..

THE THREE HOBOES FROM HOBOKEN, { Ben Thayer,.... Howland Yell,.. Hooper Upp,...

THE NEGRO SERVANT, Cole Black, out for the dust——with a duster,..

THE GOOD SHEPHERD, Rev. Goodas Canby,................

THE SWEET CORRESPONDENT, Adeline More,............

THE SHY COQUETTE, Lotta Fellers,.........................

THE GAY COMPANION, Helena Bandbox,...................

THE ONLY ONE, Elizabeth Unit, doing the natives as "Miss Fitt,"...

WHY WE LOWER THE CURTAIN.

Act I.—Lobby of the Porter House, the summer hotel at Brights-ville-on-the-Hudson. "The City Crowd on A Summer Outing."

Act II.—The inventor's room at the Porter House. "The promise repudiated."

Act III.—In Florida, the Land of Flowers. "The Village Crowd on A Summer Outing." Tableau I.——Vestibule of the Mugg Mansion, on the banks of the St. Johns River. Morning. Tableau II.——Mugg Mansion's vestibule, on the St. Johns River's banks. Afternoon. Tableau III.——On the banks of the River St. Johns' Vestibule of the Mansion of the Mugg's. Evening.

Act II.

Office of the Porter House, the Summer Hotel.

[At rise, the Three Hoboes from Hoboken discovered seated in office, while Herrmann P. reads newspaper behind desk.]

Hooper Upp: [Looking up from paper he, also, is reading,] I see by th' "Bugle" thet it's gittin' so all-fired hot an' dry in some parts o' th' kentry, thet there wunt nothin' grow this year. Now ef——

Herrmann: [Leaning elbows on desk.] Shiminy Ghris'mas! Vy, dot don'dt vos somedings ad all, mine gind friendts. Vy, in some bortions off der Vest, dot croundt iss alvays so try undt baked undt hardt dot nodings vill grow in any lengt' off dimes, much less ein year, ain'dt id?

Ben Thayer: [In a piping voice.] Well, ef I owned enny land like that, I'd irrigate!

[Hooper and Howland immediately spring up, sieze Ben and drag him toward sample-room.]

Hoop. and Howl.: He said he'd irrigate! He said he'd irrigate: Come on, Herrmann, we're goin' t' th' bar' t' irrigate.

Ben: (Pulling back) Say, I meant irrigate th' land; I didn't hev no idee uv——

Hoop. and Howl.: (All returning to seats,) Oh, yew make us tired.

Her.: I tell you vot I doo, poys: I fill shoodt dot irrigation for dot crowd——

(T. H., not waiting for him to finish, rising similtaniously, and come down two steps, saying proudly)

T. H.: We're the three hoboes, and we can't refuse a drink.

Her, (Finishing.)——Off one off you vill lendt me a dime. I vas a leedle shordt off cash, don'dt id?

T. H. (Immediately flop into chairs and snore loudly.) (Enter Fuller Tawk. He bustles up to desk, slaps valise down on the floor, and rests hands lightly on counter.)

Fuller Tawk: Is this the hotel proprietor?

Her: Yets, sir. Vot gould I doo for mienselluf?

Fuller: B-b-b-r-r! Well, I am here on business. In the first place, sir, in the first place, my name is Fuller Tawk, and I'm a lawyer, sir, a lawyer from the city, and——

Her: [Hurriedly.] Cheese undt grackers! A lawyer? Choost oxcoose me for ein moment!

[He turns and removes watch and other articles of value from person, and places in safe, carefully locking latter. Then again iurns to Ful., who has been reading newspaper.]

Her: Now, Meester Dalk, I vos retty soo——

Ful: B-b-b-r-r-r! I understand, sir, I understand. And now to procede. I will come to the point at once. I am here in the vilage of Brightsville in search of a man by the name of Prof. Lectric Carr. Do you know of any such person?

Her: Prof. Legtrig Garr? Vell, dot soundts gind off familiarity, bud I gouldn't recollect chust now anyvon by dot names. But vy doo I atsk?

Fuller: I'll tell you the whole story, sir, the whole story, because you may be able to supply me with valuable information. You see an eccentric old bachelor by the name of Earnest Mugg died, a short time ago, in New York city, leaving a very peculiar will, sir, a very peculiar will. Now by the conditions of the said will, a certain Otto Sight and a certain——But to save time, I may as well read you the will itself, of which I have an exact copy· [Produces legal-looking document.] B-b-b-r-r-r! Now, the last will and testament of the late Earnest Mugg is as follows, my dear sir, precisely as follows:

"First, I do hereby give, devise and bequeath to the Fat Men's Club of New York, the sum of one thousand dollars in gold, to be used in furnishing the apartments of that order. |

"Second, I do hereby reserve and set aside ten thousand dollars for the establishment and promotion of an Independent Society for the Prevention of Cruelty to Old Bachelors; the said society to consist only of unmarried men, and its aim to be, as its name implies, the prevention of the malicious persecution of old bachelors by young and heartless females.

"And last, I do hereby give, devise, and bequeath the entire residue of all my property and possessions, real, personal, and mixed, of what nature and kind soever, and wheresoever the same shall be at the time of my death, to the one of my two nephews, Otto Sight and Prof. Lectric Carr, an inventor, who shall first win the hand and heart of my first, last, and only female friend, Miss Elizabeth Unit, of New York city; each of the above-named nephews, Otto Sight and Prof. Lectric Carr, to leave·efore paying addresses to the lady, on A Summer Outing with a small party, for recreative and rejuvenating purposes, within the first summer season which shall follow my decease. In case Miss Unit should refuse for any reason whatsoever, be it love, duty, or otherwise that prompts her, to marry either of my said nephews, the entire residue of all my property, real, personal, and mixed, shall be equally divided among the several charitable institutions of New York City."

[Ful. slaps will, folds up, and returns to pocket.)

Ful: There! That is essentially the entire will, though the old gentleman went on to name his executors, etc. But you will now understand, sir, you will now understand why I am in search of Prof. Lectric Carr. To all of my knowledge, this person has not yet heard of the death of his uncle, or the provisions of the will; nor are his exact whereabouts known to the executors. And I, sir, I, Fuller Tawk, being commissioned by the said executors to search for and find him, am therefore and for that reason now present in the village of Brightsville. From numerous skillful inquiries, I have acquired the knowledge that though in his extreme youth he was a resident of New York City, he rambled considerably, and when last heard of was in this village. Now, my dear sir, have you any idea where I may find him?——And to speak the truth, do you really know of any such person as Prof. Lectric Carr?

Her: (Pondering.) Brodefressor Legtrig Garr, eh? Garr! Garr! Garr! Led me t'ought abowid dot! Dere vos Freight Garr, undt Shleebing Garr, undt Dining Garr, undt Vestibul Garr, undt Fladt Garr—— Oh-h, yaa! Py Chim! Dit you vos saidt he iss ein infentor?

Ful: So the will states. But have——

Her: Den I kess I vos got him logated. Dere iss a cerdain gurious guss in Prightsfille who iss chenerally known as "Flat" Garr, undt he iss ein infentor. Flat Garr,—— galled "Flat" on aggount off hiss bocket-boog. So he must pe your man. I dink me I rememper, now, off hiss vonce delling me hiss name Legdrig Garr iss. You see, he hass hiss shob in dot room right abofe der offitce, here, undt he bays for id py gifing me shmall bud useful infentions, undt——

(At this moment Hall Work rushes in with telegram, and exits.)

Her: (Opening envelope.) A delegram! Cheese undt grackers! I wonter who dis gan pe from. (Reads.) "With party of three, will be at your place on 9:30 train on A Summer Outing. Reserve sooms. - Signed, Otto Sight."

Ful: (Exitedly.) Otto Sight! Why, that's one of the nephews named in the will, and a cousin to Lectric Carr. So he's coming here on the Summer Outing required in the will, eh? (Consults watch.) Great Scott! The 9:30 train is due here in a very short time. It will be necessary for me to notify the inventor quickly, so that he may have an equal opportunity with the other fellow. You say this Flat Carr, as you call him, rooms right above this office?

Her: Yets, sir.

Ful: And is he at this moment in his room?

Her: Vell, I supbose he iss, bud he nefer allows himself soo pe disturbed ven he iss voiking. Now, he vill pe town bretty guick, alretty, undt maype you petter vait a leedle, don'dt id?

Ful: Well, well, I'll go out and have a look at your village, and will be back soon. He'll be down in half an hour, I suppose?

Her: Yaa, I kess so.

Ful: Well, I'll leave my grip here, then, till I return. I thank you very much for the important information you have given me, my dear sir, and I tell you truly, sir, truly, that it is through you alone that I have at last located the inventor, for I had almost dispaired of ever finding him. It's all right.——I'll see him through.

(Exit Fuller, L.)

Her: Oh, you vos extirely velcome soo dot informations. (Aside) I'll chust charch him oop mid dot ven I gif him his pill. (Makes a note of it.) Say, vake oop, you vellers, (to T. H,) undt carry oop stairs dose trunks vot vos chust gome for yesterday's arrifals. (T. H. snore loudly.)

[Fuller Tawk steps out of L.]

Ful. Have a drink with me, boys?

(T. H. exit L., with speed.||

Herrmann, left alone, opens safe, removes watch, etc., and replaces upon person. Voices and clinking of glasses emnate from sample room, L.||

First voice, (Ben Thayer): Say, that wus a great fish story Flat Carr wuz a-tellin' last night.

Second voice, (Ful.): B-b-b-r-r-r! A new fish story? Hum! what is it?

First voice: W'y, he said he an' a frien' wuz fishin' all day Sunday an' never drinked a drop. He! he! he!.

(Loud laughs, clinking of glasses)

Her: (Looking up from paper he has been reading.) Shimmey Ghristmas! I kess me dem vellers vos a goot dimes having alretty, don'dt it? Here dey gomes now!

(Enter T. H., L, wiping lips on handkerchiefs.)

Her: Say, vere vos dot law sharp, don'dt id?

Ben Thayer: Oh, he's gone down tew see wot kind of a place that is where Flat Carr wuz a-fishin' last Sunday.

(T. H. laugh and sit down.)

Her: Consulting watch|| Vell. I vonder ven dot cidy growd

vouldt got here, alretty. Dot drain moost pe——

(Faint laugh without. Turn to door.)

Her: Py chim! You pet me my life I dink dot iss der cidy growd now. I shase meinselluf oudt undt see.

(Runs to door and looks along driveway. Quick music, faint at first.)

Her: (Waveing arms) Dey vos gomin'! dey vos comin'! Here vos the cidy crowd on a Summer Outing!

(T. H. rush outside. Music loud. Laughter and voices loud. Hall Work comes in wheeling little trunk on big truck. Throws trunk in L. door—great crash of glass—then follows in with the truck. Enter the City Crowd, led by Otto Sight, the Hoboes and Herrmann following. Her. goes behind desk and turns on electric stud in shirt bosom. Hoboes crowd about the newcomers.)

Otto Sight: (Removing cigar from mouth) Well, we're at last. Have you——

Miss Fitt: (Pushing him aside.] Yes, we are here. Particularly myself. I am here. How's the boy?

Her: Eh? Vot poy?

M. F: Where are our rooms?

Her: Dey vos all retty, I dinks, ain'dt id? Yaa, I kess so.

M.F: Well, how about the boy?

Her: Der poy!

M .F: Yes, the boy.

Her: Vell, vot vos I dalkin' abowit, anyhow?

M.F: (As she walks around and gets a sight of sign, "Whistle Parlor," over bar-room door.) Well, what in the world does that sign mean? I never saw anything like it in my life before, and I've lived right in the city ever since I was a child.

[During conversation, exit T.H., L.

Her: Oh, dot? Vy, dot iss der Vistle Barlor, vere dose guests vet deir vistles. Dot names iss von off Flat Garr's infentions.

M.F: Flat Carr! Oh, is that the boy?

Her: Vell, he—— Now see here, I don'dt know any poy! Undershoodt dot! Flat Garr iss really Brodefressor Leg——

(Explosion above, cracking of plaster and dropping of laths. Prof. Lectric Carr drops through forced hole in ceiling, and lands upon office floor. Enter T.H., L. Silence for a moment, during which time, Prof. glances fitfully about.)

Prof. Lectric Carr: Well, that's the time I took a drop too much!

(He is pulled to feet.)

The Girls: Oh, my! is he hurt?—Is he seriously injured? Will he recover? etc., etc., etc.

Her: For gootness sake, Flat, wot vos dot oxplosions?

Prof: I was just experimenting with my latest invention for preventing a woman from talking a man to death when he is reading his newspaper. The theme was too strong for the apparatus and the thing exploded.

The Ladies: [In chorus.] Oh, you horrid man!

Her: Mein cracious, Brodefressor, was you hurdt,

Prof: Hurt! Well, no; I think not.

Her: Dit dot oxplosions do much tamage py dot room oppstairs?

Prof: Well, I don't know. I was in such a hurry when I came down that I didn't stop to see. I'll go up and find out, right away.

[Exit, stairway, to snare-drum beats.]

Otto: [Staring after him in astonishment, as do the rest of the City Crowd.] Well, who, in the name of goodness, is that queer old freak?

Her: Oh, dot vos Legtrig Garr, der infentor. [Ot. starts.] He hass oxplosions abowit dwice a veek. alretty. Vy, only day pefore yetstiddy, he plowed in some money, undt——

Ot: Well, all right, all right; you don't need to talk all day about the old fool. Give us our rooms. We're slightly tired after our long journey from the city, and want a chance to rest, while you are only making us more fatigued.

Her: Vell, you don't need soo get so madt abowit id. (Taps bell.]

M.F: Oh, don't mind him. He's positively the most disagreeable man I ever met.

[Enter Hall Work, L.]

Her: Here, poy, show——

M.F: Oh, is this the boy? Why, hello, boy. Why, isn't he a nice boy!

Her: Say, I vish you vould gif me some rest on dot poy qusiness; I don'dt gould understoodt dot ad. Hall, all you hake dese beople oop soo deir rooms. I haf put dem all on der nort' side off der house. Dey are so fresh I vos me afraidt dey vouldt shpoil if dey vos put vhere it varm iss. (Hands him keys, taps bell vigorously.) Now, shkip avay quick oudt, alretty.

(Hall starts toward stairway, followed by the City Crowd, with the exception of Adeline More, who lingers for a moment at the desk.)

Adeline: (Confidingly) If there are any letters for me in the next mail, be sure to send them up, Mr. Pumpernickel, for, though I am only a mere child, (archly) I carry on a large city correspondence.

[She laughs. Hurries back in time to catch others at foot of stairs. Lotta Fellers then tiptoes to desk with finger on lips.]

Lotta: Oh, do you know, Mr. Proprietor, I do so want to ask

you one little question: Are there any nice young men about the hotel?

Her; ‖Grinning broadly.‖ You pet my life I know some nice young men.

Lot   Oh, I'm so glad! Nice young men are absolutely necessary to my existence;——they sort of liven up things, you know.   (Laughs giddily, and exit, stairs.)

Her: Any nice young men, eh? Vell, dot gifs me a chance, ain'dt id? Py Chim! bud dot girl vos——
[Enter Ful., rear.]

[Her. again removes watch and chain and places in safe. Then siezes broom and sweeps away debris from explosion.]

Ful: B-b-b-r-r-r! My German friend, have you seen anything of Prof. Lectric Carr, of whom I am in search?

Her: Yets, sir. He dropped in chust a foo minutes ago. I kess he pe pack preddy guick, ain'dt id?

Ful: Very well, my dear sir, very well. Did you mention to him any hint of——

[Just then a sharp whistle and tapping of cane is heard on stair-landing above, and out of sight.]

Her: Dot's der Brodefressor now. [Calling.] Vell, vot it iss?

Voice from Stairway [Prof.]: The explosion didn't hurt anything. The music seems to be all sound, the butter's as strong as ever, and the safe's safe.

Her: All righdt. Fall down stairs; dere's a man here to see you.
[Prof. comes down and stands on lower landing.]

Prof: What is it? More people about money.

Ful: Precisely, sir, precisely. More people about money. How did you guess it so well?

Prof: Well, who are you?

Ful: My name is Fuller Tawk, sir, Fuller Tawk, and I am a lawyer from the city.

Prof: A lawyer! Excuse me a moment!

[Orch. plays strain from "Johnny Fill Up the Bowl", and Prof. marches out, L. Repeats, and he re-enters, wiping lips on sleeve.‖

Prof: ‖Holding up hands.‖ I left my pocket-book up on the time table. Whose bill are you hired to collect?

Ful: You misunderstand my mission, sir, you do, really. I am here not to collect money, but to——
‖Enter Ot., st'w'y. Taps Ful.'s arm.‖

Ot: Hum! Excuse me, gentlemen. Mr. Tawk, I never had the honor of an introduction to you, but I know you just the same, and I take the liberty of asking your company in a little sight-seeing trip about the village.

Ful: ‖Coldly.‖ I have already viewed all the points worth visiting.

Ot: Then allow me to suggest a cocktail.

Ful: B-b-b-r-r-r! It would be an insult to refuse your invitation. Excuse me, Mr. Carr, I will return presently and resume the conversation we have begun.

[Exit Ot. and Ful., L.]

Her: [Gazing after.] I pet my life dot Oddo Sight vos chust dryin' soo keep dot lawyer from dellin' der Brodefressor abowit dot vill as long as he gan, so as to finish his Summer Ouding pefore Flat knows anydings abowit id. (To Prof.) Dot Oddo Sight vos so disacreeable dot efery dimes he gomes into der offitce, he gifs me a goldt chill. Donnerwetter! I wos got one now.

Prof: Well, come right over to the register and get warm. Say, gimme a cigar.

Her: Vell, I—— Here gomes der poys.

[Enter T. H., rear.]

Ben: Well. we're in trouble ag'in, by crickey!

Her: Vell, vot iss der madder now?

Ben Thayer: The lease on the house we're livin' in hez run out and we can't find another house t' suit us.

Her: Iss dot all, I kess me I gan fix you oudt, ain'dt id? Brodefessor, dese fellers vant a house.

Prof: Well, all right, what kind of a house do they want?

[Goes behind desk and prepares to write in register .]

Her: He says vot kindt of a house do you vant. Do you vant a white house or a green house?

Ben: A white house like Bill McKinley's.

Prof: [Repeats. writing.) A white house.

Her: Vill you haf der roof on top off der house?

Ben: Yes.

Prof: Shingles on the outside, I s'pose?

Her: Yets, shingles on der oudtside. And do you want square rooms?

Ben: Yes.

Her: Square rooms, Flat.

Porf; Does he want three or four walls to the square rooms?

Ben. Four walls, and I want movable doors.

Her. Movable doors. Do you vant the doors to swing o n hinges?

Ben: Yes.

Her: Doors to swing on hinges. Will you have windows with or without glass!

Ben: I'd like to have glass in the windows.

Her: He vants glass in der windows, Flat.

Prof: Transparent glass, I s'pose?

Her; Yets . Vell, dot's all.

Ben: When kin we have the house?

Prof: It will be done in five minutes. Do you want it delivered or will you take it with you!

Ben; Oh, we will take it with us.

Prof: Well, all right. I'll take it over now.

(Exit Prof., L.)
(Enter the girls.)

Lotta: Oh, we've found our rooms to be just too perfectly lovely for anything. But if there were only some nice young men here now, I should like it ever so much better.

Adeline: And I shall never be perfectly happy here until my mail begins to arrive from the city.

Miss Fitt: Well that's just the way with Lotta; she won't be happy until her male begins to arrive from the city, but she's not very particular. She'll take any old male, whether he's from the city or not.

Lotta: Why, you horrid thing! I think you're real mean.

(Enter Prof., L., with invention.)

Prof: Herrmann, gimme a cigar.

Her: Nein.

Prof: Yes, nine'll do.

Her: You vos not misundershtood me. Haf you got der money soo bay for dot cigar?

Prof: Well, that depends. How much are they worth?

Her: Two dollars undt a helluf a biece. Dese are free silfer cigars.

Prof: Two dollars and a half a piece? Well, how much do you charge for a whole one?

Her: Eh! Vot dit I saidt?

Prof: Yes. Well, do I get a cigar?

Her; Vell, I shouldt say nodt.

Prof: I don't get a cigar! Now look here, Herrmann Pumpernickel, if I don't get a cigar, I'll blow this hotel to smithereens with my new patent invention, loaded with explosive for blasting reputations. Here goes!

(Places machine on desk and begins turning canks, wheels, etc]

Her: Loog oudt! He vos goin' soo shoot!

(Girls all scream, everyone exits quick as possible.)

Prof: (Calmly helping himself to double handful cigars from box on desk. And I get a cigar!   (Exit, L.,)

(One by one, the T. H., the girls, and Her. cautiously re-enter. Her. finds empty cig. box.)

Her: Oh, I see id all now, Dat iss annuder off Fladt Garr's chokes. [Laughs,] He got der cigar.

[Enter Prof. and Ful.,L.]

Ful: Now that I've gotten rid of that obnoxious Otto Sight, now that I've gotten rid of him, I wish to procede with the matter we were speaking about before. In the presence of all these witnesses, Prof. Lectric Carr, I state that I am here to volunteer you the information that your uncle, Earnest Mugg, died in New York

City, a short time ago, leaving a very peculiar will; and if you are
the first of two nephews to comply with the provisions of the will,
you are the possible heir to a million dollars!

[Prof. says nothing, but falls over against wall. Ful. pulls him
up.]

Prof: [After silence.] Well,what are the provisions of the will?

Ful: B-b-b-r-r-r! I have here an exact copy of the document,
and it will be a great saving of valuable time for you to read it
over yourself.   (Hands will to Prof.]

Prof: This is very finely written...I can't see to read it.....
What'll I do?....Oh, yes.

(Walks to ice-water tank, strikes match, looks up.)   '

Prof: I'll light the gas and see.

(Lights water faucet. Silence.]

Prof: The first paragraph doesn't refer to me, neither does the
second. Here it is: (Reads.) "And last, I do hereby give,
devise and bequeath the entire residue of all my property and
possessions, real, personal, and mixed, of what nature and kind"
soever and wheresoever the same shall be at the time of my
death, to the one of my two nephews, Otto Sight, or Professor
Lectric Carr, an inventor, who shall first win the heart and hand
of my first, last and only female friend, Miss Elizabeth Unit, of
New York City, each of the above named nephews, Otto Sight
and Lectric Carr, to leave before paying addresses to the lady on a
Summer Outing, with small party, for recreative and rejuvinat-
ing purposes, within the first summer season which shall follow
my decease." (He looks up.) Is this Otto Sight named in the
will the same man who is at this hotel on A Summer Outing?

Ful: He is.

Prof: And does this thing mean that I've got to get married to
a certain woman in New York before the other fellow?

Ful: That's precisely what it does mean, my dear sir.

Prof:(Abruptly turning and handing back will.) Well, then
I'm not in it.

[Everyone springs up and rushes down.]

Chorus: What! Arn't you going to try for the million dollars?

Prof: No, not if I have to marry in order to get it. It's worth
every cent of the fortune to have to live with a woman.

The Girls: Oh, you horrid thing!....I'd like to scratch your
eyes out!....Let me get at him!

Ben: [Piping up.] Wal, ef I wuz in your position an' hed them
kind 'o conditions a-starin' me in th' face, I wouldn't let no pesky
city chap walk off with the gal an' th' fortune 'thout makin' a fight
fer it.

Her: Undt me neider. Flat, I vos ashamed off yer.

T. H: [Together.] We're the Three Hoboes from Hoboken,

and tew uphold th' repertashun uv Brightsville, we demand that yew enter th' race fer th' million dollars.

Prof: ‖With determination.‖ No. It's no use. I won't do it.

(T. H. stare at one another and nod. Then turn to Her.)

(Enter Ot., and sits.)

Her: Cheese undt grackers! Vy, dot man vos shust so shtubborn lige a shassack. Now, off he vould go in undt peat dot summer shpordt, it vould pe der pest advertisements dot Prightsfille efer hadt. Der name vould pe in all dot bapers, undt der Borter House vould doo pusiness mit tourists lige a house afire. (Gets watch and hat.) I vos goin' soo dink vot I gan doo abowit dot.

(Exit Her.,rear.)

Lot: Oh, girls, I do wish I could find some of those nice young men Mr. Pumpernickel promised me. What shall we do to kill time?

Ad: And it's so queer that I havn't yet received any letters. Oh, do lets do something to pass away time till evening, when we can go riding on the Hudson.

[Specialties for twenty minutes]

‖After specialties, Her. enters and bustles up to Prof.‖

Her; Vell, I haf ad ladst decided what soo doo. Off you vould get ahegdt off dot cidy fellers dere, undt win dot cidy gerrul undt dot fortunes, it vouldt pe der pest advurtisements for Prightsfille undt der summer hotel vot ever vos: for as a guest of der Porter House, you vould pe known der gountry aroundt. Now, I atsk you once more, vill you dry soo scoop in der maichen undt dot gelt?

Prof: I think I answered that question once before. No; I'd rather be a single inventor without a cent, than a multi-milionire with a wife.

The Ladies: Oh, isn't he just horrid!

Her; Dot seddles id. It vos got soo peen done.

‖Peculiar music. Enter Three Hoboes, arm in arm. They advance a letter to Prof.‖

Ben Thayer; ‖In sepulchral tones.‖ Here's a communication from the pen of a Long Neglected Genius. Read!

‖Prof. grasps letter with trembling hands, opens it, and then staggers back with a hollow moan.‖

Prof: It's all over, This musty, cob-webbed old claim must be satisfied. Boys, I will win the city girl if I die in the attempt.

CURTAIN.

Miss Fitt; What is this all powerful message which you will marry to satisfy?

Prof: A bill of twelve years' standing from my tailor.

CURTAIN.

Act II.

[Interior of the Inventor's Room at the Porter House.]

(At rise, Enter Fuller Tawk and the Professor.)

Fuller Tawk: Now, my dear sir, as long as this Otto Sight is already here taking the Summer Outing required in the will, it behooves you to move quickly, if you wish to come out ahead and become the possessor of the fortune and the girl. Now I make bold to ask you, sir, I make bold to ask you, where do you intend to go on your Summer Outing?

Prof: (Motioning Fuller to take a chair, takes one himself.] Is this young lady, Miss Elizabeth Unit, in New York City at the present time?

Ful: She is, to the best of my knowledge, sir.

Prof: [Emphatically.] Then I'll go to New York. Otto Sight came from New York to Brightsville on his Summer Outing, I'll go from Brightsville to New York on mine, and the young lady, being in the latter place, I'll do all I can towards winning her regard, before the other fellow can get back to the city.

Ful: (Both, rising, and he vigorously slapping Prof. upon the back.) Good! good! good! It's an excellent plan, sir, an excellent plan, and I wish you the greatest of success. Now I've taken a queer dislike to that fellow, Otto Sight, and I advise you to start on your outing, my dear sir, as soon as you can,——today, if possible,—— for I have a feeling that if he cannot win the fortune by fair means, he will certainly attempt to win it by foul. Well, as I said before, I wish you the greatest of success, (Picking up hat and edging toward rear door.) the greatest of success, and——

(Her. is heard outside, puffing and blowing.)

Voice: Shiminy Ghristmas! Vot negxt, alretty, don'dt id?

(Enter Her., mopping face with hankch'f.)

Her: Oxcoose me, shentlemens, bud I vos got some oxtonishing news. Who you dinks vos shust arrifed ad dis hotel on A Summer Oudting?

Ful: We have not the least idea, Mr. Pumpernickel, not the least idea in the world. Who is it, the Prince of Wales, or ...... [Insert name of some prominent city man.]

Her: Id vos der oldt womans named in der oldt bachelor's vill, Miss Elizabeth Unit, off New York!

Prof. and Ful: What!

(Fuller stands as if turned to stone, while Prof. tumbles back into a peculiar looking machine.)

Ful: Are you sure about this?

Her: Shust so sure as I gould pe. But now I got me soo go down undt see dot she gets her room all rightd. I got me so oxcited ven I foundt oudt who she vos, dot I runnedt oop here shust so guick as I could, alretty.   [Exit Her., rear.]

[Fuller and Prof. stare at each other for a moment,‖

Prof: ‖Extricating himself.) Well, what do you think about this?

Ful: B-b-b-r-r-r! Well, it is a surprise. I must say. And besides, my dear sir, besides, it entirely reverses the condition of affairs. As things now stand. Mr. Carr. if you go to New York on your Summer Outing, Miss Unit will be left here at Brightsville, a victim to the wiles of Otto Sight: and then, sir, then where will your chances be?

‖Both take seats.‖

Prof: Well, I don't know. It's a queer thing to me how that women happened to take a Summer Outing, and above all how she came to Brightsville to take it. What are we going to do about it?

Ful: B-b-b-r-r-r! My dear sir, this is very confusing, very confusing. indeed. But give me a few moments to think over it, and I may be able to offer a feasible, suggestion, sir, a feasible suggestion.

(Exit Ful. and Prof., left.)

(Enter Otto Sight.]

Otto: By Jove! Fortune seems to be playing directly into my hands. Now that Elizabeth Unit has arrived from New York on Summer Outing, I will not have to return to New York to woo her, but can accomplish my purpose right here at this summer resort, while my inventive cousin, whom I never saw till I arrived at Brightsville, will be forced, in order to comply with the conditions of the will, to stay at some other resort, for a short time, on his Summer Outing. I think I can defeat him without an effort, for besides the advantage I will gain by his being absent, his appearance is something frightful; while I, I pride myself in saying, am fairly a handsome man. And though I have not seen her yet, I imagine that Elizabeth Unit isn't a bad-looking personage herself. Yes, I think I can win both her and the fortune without the least shade of difficulty. Well, I'll go down to the office and see if I can get a glimpse of the future Mrs. Otto Sight. (Ex. Ot., re.)

(Enter Ful. and Prof., L.)

Ful: (Excitedly.) By Jove, Professor, I've solved the problem! Congratulate me, sir, congratulate me, I have solved the problem! ‖Cooling down, seats himself.‖ B-b-b-r-r-r! Yes, my dear sir, I have formulated a plan by which you may, at least, hold an even chance with Otto Sight, though you certainly will not have any advantage over him.

Prof: ‖Showing interest.‖ Is that so? Well, that's good news. What's your plan?

Ful: B-b-b-r-r-r! Well, I'll tell you. In the first place, sir, in the first place, I have discovered a flaw in the will.

Prof: A flaw!

Ful: Yes, a flaw.

Prof: Oh, a flaw.

Ful. Of course, a flaw. And I will read you the passage in which the flaw occurs: (Reads from will.) "...Each of my above nephews, Otto Sight and Prof. Lectric Carr, to leave, before paying addresses to the lady, on A Summer Outing with small party. ....", etc., etc. Now, my dear sir, the will simply says to LEAVE on A Summer Outing, and nothing is mentioned at all, sir, to show how long the outing must last Now, this is a point that the disagreeable Otto Sight must have overlooked, else he would not be in Brightsville at this moment; and I pride myself, sir, I pride myself that none but a lawyer—and a good one, at that—would have discovered that flaw.

Prof: Well, I don't see how that flaw, as you call it, is going to benefit me any.

Ful. You don't? B-b-b-r-r-r! Well I will explain. Now, as long as the will simply says to "leave" on a Summer Outing, what is to prevent you from boarding the train here at Brightsville in company with your Three Hoboes, as you call them,—to make the small party, you know—board the train here at Brightsville, and getting off at the next station, return by the special that arrives here in thirty minutes. In that manner you will comply with the provisions of the will, by leaving on a Summer Outing, yet immediatly coming back, so as to put yourself on an equal footing with Otto Sight, as far as Miss Elizabeth Unit is concerned. Do you grasp my meaning, my dear sir?

Prof: Well I should say yes. I grasp it. That's a good scheme, I'll carry it out at once, And if I don't win that fortune, it won't be because I havn't tried.

Ful: That's the way to talk, my dear sir, that's the way to talk, Now, I've taken a decided liking to you, professor, and I hope you will come out with flying colors. But I advise you to act at once,—today, within an hour, if possible— for remember that Otto Sight is from the city and is as smooth as an eel. Well, now 1 must be going. 1 will stop in the lobby and persuade the Three Hoboes from Hoboken to accompany you on your abbreviated Summer Outing, so as to make the small party required in the will. And remember, act at once. 1t's all right,——1'll see you through!

[Exit Ful., rear.]

Prof: Yes, I will act at once....1 wonder if that girl is pretty ....1 hope she is....1 wish I could see her....1 wonder if she'll fall in love with me at sight?....Well I'll have to get ready to go on my Summer Outing.

[Removes his coat, revealing a red flannel shirt, with false white bosom. Rolls up his sleeves, goes to a corner, mixes lather, applies it to his face, and prepares to shave. Leisurely he takes the razor, when feminine laughs are heard without. Prof. pauses abruptly and gazes fitfully about.)

Prof: Really, I believe some one is coming.

‖Listens. Laughter becomes louder. Voices.‖

Prof: I can't let them see me like this. Where'll I hide? Oh, yes! (Runs quickly behind fancy screen.)

‖Enter Miss Fitt, Lotta and Adeline.‖

Lotta: ‖Beginning before entrance of trio.‖ Oh, it's so embarrassing isn't it, girls, when you are alone with your beau for the first time?

Adeline: Indeed I haven't found it so.

Miss Fitt: You haven't?

Adeline: Not at all. My beau talks all the time, and doesn't give me a chance to feel embarrassed.

Lotta: He is a good talker, then.

Adeline: Well, I should say so, he's a barber.

(More laughter.)

M. F: [Lightly.] Well, I havn't any beau myself, so I don't know much about it.

The Others: Why, you poor girl!

[Prof. peeks cautiously over top of screen.]

Prof: I wish I had a bow. I'd shoot somebody. Really. I wish they'd get out of here. My train leaves in fifteen minutes, and if I don't hurry up, I'll get left.

(Adeline turns toward him, and he pops down out of sight again.)

Ad: So this is the old inventor's shop! What queer contrivances he has about.

M. F: Yes, and what an artistic screen that once was, over yonder.

The Others: Oh, yes, isn't it lovely!

(They all walk up and examine it.)

The Girls: It's so attractive!....Yes, and such a pretty figure is embroidered in it!....How beautiful!

Lot: Say, girls, I wonder if there's a figure on the other side

M. F: Well, lets find out.

[Screen jumps up and down, unnoticed.]

The Girls: Of course we will.

‖Start to go behind screen, when latter suddenly moves to middle. They scream and come down quickly.‖

Lot: Oh, girls, th-there m-must be s-something alive b-behind that s-screen!

,Prof. thrusts head through screen, looks around.|
Prof: There is.
[Girls scream again.]
The Girls: It's a man! It's a man! 'Oh, the awful thing!
|;Exit rear,
Prof: (Coming from behind screen.) Yes, there WAS a figure
on the other side. I don't know what that Lotta Fellers ran
away for. She was just crazy for a nice young man. Well, I guess
I'll have to hurry up. |Puts on his coat.| I won't have time to
shave.
(Enter Fuller, briskly)
Ful: (During this speech, Prof. wipes lather from his face.)
B-b-b-r-r-r! My dear professor, you must hurry. Why, your
train will leave in ten minutes, and you have yet to get to the
station. Remember sir, remember, that if you miss this train
you will be forced to wait until tomorrow to start on your Summer Outing, and will in that way give Otto Sight a great advantage, for the will states, you remember, that you are not to pay
your addresses to the lady before—
Prof: Well, all right. I'll start right now. We'll be back in
half an hour on the special. Well, au revoir.
(Exit Prof., rear. Fuller takes seat.)
Ful: Well he's a queer old chap, certainly, that inventor, but
still, I've taken a strange liking to him in spite of his eccentri-
city.
[Enter Miss Fitt, softly.]
Miss Fitt: [As she stands in doorway.] And so have I.
[Fuller whirls about in chair.]
Ful: |Rising politely.| B-b-b-r! Ah! Miss Fitt, so it is you, is
it? Won't you be seated.
M. F: Well, I don't care if I do.
Ful: I believe you coincided with me when I unconsiously
uttered aloud the statement of my liking for Prof. Lectric Carr.
Miss Fitt: I did. And for some reason, I have taken an equally
strange dislike to Otto Sight, the leading member of our Summer
Outing party.
Ful; You have? Why, very oddly, I have taken just such a
dislike to him myself.
Miss Fitt: Really?
Ful: Yes, and I've formulated a great idea to help the Prof. win
this fortune he is after.
Miss Fitt; Is that so! What is it?
Ful: Well, just step into the conservatory with me and I'll
tell you the whole scheme. The Prof. is even now gone carry-
ing out the idea. It's all right,—I'll see him through.
(Exit F. and M. F., L,)
(Enters Otto Sight,)

Ot: That lawyer seems to be working with all his might to help Flat Carr. That was a very shrewd scheme of his to take advantage of the flaw in the will, but little advantage will it ever give the inventor. Now, I pumped the Dutchman for all he was worth, and I find that Carr is to start on his Summer Outing, but will be back here again in a very small fraction of an hour. Very shrewd, very shrewd, indeed. However, the idea is only to put him on an equal footing with myself, so I have no cause to complain. Let me see. In a few minutes he will be back from his extended Summer Outing, and he will begin at once, I suppose, to pay his addresses to the girl. But I'll take her out of his way long enough to persuade her to marry me. How shall I manage it? Ah, yes. I'll organize a small fishing party, include Elizabeth Unit, and before the return of the inventor we shall be a number of miles distant from Brightsville. Then, in some shady glen, I can make love to my heart's content,—and then ho! for a wife and fortune, and the defeat of my eccentric cousin!

[Exit Ot., rear.]

(Enter M. F. and Ful.)

Ful: B-b-b-r-r-r! So there, Miss Fitt, you have my idea in a nutshell.

M. F: Yes, and a good one it is, too, Mr. Tawk. If it were not for that idea, Mr. Carr would indeed be placed at a great disadvantage. But Otto Sight, I suppose, knows nothing of this ruse?

Ful: Well, it really doesn't make much difference whether he knows it or not. The Professor will be back here in a short time, and he will have an equal chance with his cousin, so there would be no harm done even if he should know it. Oh, it's all right,— —I'll see him through! ‖Exit Ful., L.‖

M. F: [In soliloquoy.] Oh, dear, I wish this was over. [She slowly crosses room.] I do think Helena keeps too much to herself. She should push matters as quickly as possible. Well, for that matter, my own sense of like and dislike leads me to believe that the inventor is the most honorable of the two cousins and the most worthy of my hand, although he seems to have little liking for females; but I must wait until something comes up that will enable me to view each of the men in his own true character. I shall be glad when it is all over.

(Ensemble specialty.)

‖After spec., M. F., Lot., Ad., Her., and Ful. remain.‖

Her: [Enthusiastically.] Miss Fidt, you vos got a foice chust so sofdt undt shveedt like a crow's, alretty, undt I vos sharmed mit your singing. Der only equal I gan dink off, soo your lofey v arbling iss a shveet-toned shteam galliope, eh, don'dt id?

M. F: Well, Mr. Pumpernickel, I am surprised at you. Why, not even that fresh young Otto Sight would talk to me like that.

No; whether Otto Sight——

[Enter Ot., rear.]

Ot: (Standing in doorway.) Ah! Excuse me for intruding, but didn't I just hear some one utter my name?

M. F: (Cooly.) Why, no; I think not.   I was simply remarking that the weather is out o' sight.   (Lot. and Ad. snicker.)

Ot: Yes, the weather is rather fine. And for that very reason ‖He winks.‖ I have decided to make up a small fishing party. To tell the truth, that's precisely why I came in just now. I would like to know if you ladies will honor me by accompanying me on the expedition.

Lot. and Ad: Oh, we'll go.

M. F: Well, I won't. You're going to have Elizabeth Unit along, I suppose?

Otto: Yes, she has consented to go.

M, F. Huh-huh! Well then you expect to land big fish.

Otto: Oh, yes. Say, what do you mean? [This last suddenly as if just comprehending.]

Her: Yets, she iss mean. Off gourse you oxpects soo landt pig fish. Say, py der vay, Meester Sight, vot kindt off fishhoogs vos you goin' soo use?

Otto: (Impatiently.) Oh, just the common trout hooks.

Her: Shiminey Ghristmas! common drout hoogs? Vy dot von't do ad all. Dese iss der kindt off hoogs ve use aroundt Prightsville. (Takes an enormous hook from corner, holds it up.)

Otto: Nonsense, nonsense! Don't be a fool, We'll if we're going afishing, we'll have to start pretty soon. So you won't accompany us, Miss Fitt?

M. F: No, sir. Not by any means.

Otto: And you two gentlemen.....‖Turning to Herrmann and Fuller.‖....will you go along?

The Two Gents: (Hesitatingly.) Well, what kind of bait are you going to use?

Otto: Worms. There are women along, you know.

The Two Gents: We can't go! We can't go! We've got a previous engagement.

Otto: All right, all right. But we'll have to be going now. Come on girls. Well, so long, people.

Adeline and Lotta: Good bye! good bye! (Follow to door, laughing.)

M. F: Goodbye. Be sure not to drink all the bait before you get to the lake.

(Exit Otto and girls, rear.)

Full: Well, I think I see through Otto Sight's clever little scheme in going fishing. He has discovered that Prof. Lectric Carr is coming back immediately, and for that reason he desires to take this Elizabeth Unit to some secluded spot in order to himself make a favorable impression, while he at the same time poisons her mind against his cousin.

Miss Fitt: Yes, I'm quite sure he's an underhanded scoundrel. Lower. But he'll be misled by the supposed Elizabeth Unit just the same.

(Just then crash of glass heard without.)

Miss Fitt: (Startled.) Heavens! What can that be? ·

Her: [Cheerfully.] Flat Garr vos pack again, I kess. His face iss so homely dat efery dimes he gomes in der hotel door undt loogs ad id real hardt, der class preaks.

Miss Fitt: Is it possible! I suppose the glass feels very much broken up about it. I wonder how he got along on his Summer Outing. Lets go down and talk to him, Mr, Pumpernickel, he's so funny and eccentric, you know.

Her: All rightd. I'm vit yer. Oxcuse us, Mr. Dalk.

Ful: Certainly.   ·

(Exit H. and M. F.)

Full: Well, I've got a few things to say to Prof. Lectric Carr myself. I guess I'l have to go to see him, too. Why, here he comes now.

(Quick music. Enter Prof., carrying slate.)

[Writes industriously for a moment. Then hands slate to Ful.]

Ful: (Reading.) "I've lost my voice. Come out and help me look for it."

Ful: Well, what kind of a voice is it?

Prof: It's a bass voice, and I lost it in the basement.

(Exit Prof., rear, immediately re-entering, L.)

Ful: Well, professor, I see you're back.

Prof: Well, it's my back. If you don't like it you don't have to look at it.

Ful: I mean, I see you have returned. Did you have a nice time?

Prof: Oh, we had a lovely time. We had a grand time. Why, the agent down to the station keeps a bulldog, a cowdog, and several little calfdogs, and we couldn't get into the waiting room. Had to sit out on the platform till the train came.

Ful: Why, what did you do that for? 'Fraid on account of the dogs?

Prof: My pants are.

Ful: Pants are what?

Prof: Frayed on account of the dogs.

Ful: Well, that's too bad. But I trust your attire isn't hopelessly damaged?

Prof: Well, what's the diffirence? Havn't I got a suit of clothes for every day in the week?

Ful: Have you? I never saw you wear any other than the one you have on.

Prof: Why, yes, that's the one. Don't I wear that every day in the week?

Ful: Say, by the way, professor, what makes your clothes look so much more peculiar than they did when you went away, half an hour ago?

Prof: Why, they're shrunken. You see we were all trying to stop a runaway horse, and I got caught in the rein. Even the church bells were ringing wet. But what has Otto Sight been doing while I was taking my half-hour outing?

Ful; Ah! now we are coming down to business. B-b-b-r-r-r! Well, my dear sir, he has gone on a fishing expedition, taking along with him Lotta Fellers, Adeline More, and Elizabeth Unit.

Prof: Well, then, he's got an advantage over me, and I can't see the girl till he gets ready to come back with her.

Ful: Precisely, my dear sir, precisely. That fishing expedition is a clever scheme of his to ingratiate himself into her affections, while he at the same time fills her ears with false and damaging stories about you.

Prof: The scoundrel! But I can't do anything now till the girl gets back. Say, by the way, have you seen my latest invention, my new rainmaking machine?

Ful: Rainmaking machine? No, but I'd like to, professor. B-b-b-r-r-r! Yes, 'd like to. Where is it?

Prof: [Uncovering invention.] Now, this is the greatest invention of the present age. It's the greatest invention the world has ever seen or ever will see, and I guarantee it to produce rain inside of two seconds after it is fired. You see, first I have to insert prejectile, which is loaded with a terrible explosive called horrorite. (Inserts projectile in mouth of gun.) Then I turn this crank to raise or depress the muzzle of the gun. Two drops of this fluid [Holds up vial, and drops some of contents on gun.] sets the interior mechanism of the invention in motion. This wheel [Turning it.] ignites the powerful rain-producing projectile, and this lever, here, throws it from the gun. Now, then, off she goes! (Pulls lever. Report. Projectile leaves gun. Thunder, lightning, rain, and wind without.)

Prof: Well, that's the entire process, and you see it's raining outside now. Oh, that invention's bound to create a disturbance in the upper circles, as soon as I get it patented. But say, Mr. Tawk, you havn't got a ham sandwich in your pocket, have you? I'm hungry as a bear.

Ful: Hungry! Why, how's that? Didn't they have a dining car on the train?

Prof: Why, no; you see it was a FAST train, and they didn't

have anything to eat. I'll go and feed myself, right away.

              (Quick music. Exit Prof., L.)

Ful: B-b-b-r-r-r! That is quite an invention, to be sure. Why, it's raining harder than ever, now. ‖Glancing out of window.⌡ I guess I'll go outside and see what the outlook is for an extended storm,   [Exit Ful., L,]

    [Enter Ot., Lot., Ad., rear. All talk as they enter.)

Lot: Isn't it just awful!

Ad: Oh, it's so exasperating!

Ot: It's just my accursed luck!

Lot: To think that this horrid rainstorm should come up just as we were starting off on our fishing expedition! I'm going right up to my room and have a good hard cry over it.

Ad: Yes, just think of the lovely sport we are missing on account of this nasty shower! Oh, I'm so disappointed I'm going right up and— and— and help Lotta cry!   [Exit Ad., R.]

Ot: And think of the grand opportunity I am losing to get a dead cinch on Elizabeth Unit and the million dollars. Oh, hang the luck! Well, as far as I know, Carr is in the same fix as I am— he hasn't yet had an opportunity to speak to the girl in private. Why, she's in her room even now, and won't come out. I wonder what makes her so shy. Why, I havn't even had a chance to see her yet, and was only relying on those two fool girls to persuade her to go fishing with us. Well, I suppose I'll have to work on the square, now, and I don't think she'll prefer that homely freak to me. But for some reason everybody seems take a queer liking to the old guy, and a sort of dislike to me. That's what makes me fear for myself if he talks to her first. I wish that inventive cousin of mine would eat a cracker and blow himself up, at some very near day.

‖Deafening ripping noise without.‖

    (Enter Prof., immediately after, carrying umbrella.)

Ot: Say, what in thunder was that noise?

Prof: Noise! Why, that wasn't a noise; that was a tennis racket. But say, what do you think of my rainstorm? Ain't it a la-la?

O: YOUR rainstorm!

P: Why, yes. I did it with my little invention.

O: You did! 'Well, then that's one more I owe you.

P: Well, you'd better pay it now.

O: What's that?

P: I say, you'd better pay me now.

O: What are you talking about?

P: Didn't you borrow two dollars of me, day before yesterday?

O: Yes.

P: I was in a saloon then, wasn't I?

O: Yes, and I was in, too.

P: I know you were,—— and I was out two.

O: What do you mean? Do you think I'm not going to pay you back?

P: Why, no; I don't THINK you're not going to pay me back.

O: There you go again! Now, don't you dare to say I mean to keep your money.

P: Well, I didn't say it. I didn't say you mean to keep my money. I only said you borrowed it, that's all. So you're going to pay me back, are you?

O: Well, I intended to.

P: Yes, and two's what you got, Oh, you hooked me in for a jay that time, all right.

O: Well, don't get excited about it. You see how cool I am.

P: Well you've been in the cooler often enough, you ought to be cool.

O: That'll do, now. Shut up or I'll leather you.

P: Well, I'm strapped now. Gimme my two dollars back and I'll be all right.

O: Didn't I tell you to shut up? If you don't shut up, I'll give you one.

P: Better give me the two while you're at it. I think——

O: Say, I'm getting tired of this, Now you go take a sneak!

P: All right, where do you want to go?

O: Say if I take hold of you once, you'll wish I hadn't.

P: Well, you touched me already. I want my money back?

O: Oh, let it fly.

P; It's flown.

O: Well, what's the difference?

P: Two dollars, and I want it now.

O: Now that's plenty!

P; Well, two dollars ought to be plenty to get out of a poor man. Mr. Sight, your're a downright robber.

O: Lectric Carr, I tell you plainly, I don't like your expression.

P: All right: I'll change it. (Strikes an attitude, and changes expression of his face.)

O: Say, you're too fresh altogether. Do you know who I am?

P: Do you know who I am?

(Song, after which Ot. chases Prof. off.)
(Enter Ful. and M. F., rear.)

Ful: Ah, my dear young lady, this is a delightful rain, truly a delightful rain!

M. F: [Both sitting.] Yes, Mr. Tawk; and it's beauty lies not only in it's refreshing coolness, but also in the glorious fact that it has foiled Otto Sight in another contemptible effort to gain an underhand advantage over the professor. This storm has prevented him from taking Elizabeth Unit out fishing.

Ful: Yes, so I am aware. And a lucky thing it is, too, for our inventive friend. But there is one very ludicrous side to this situation, my dear young lady, that you do not know of or appreciate.

M. F: There is?

Ful: Yes, the real joke of the whole affair is this: Lectric Carr unwittingly manufactured that rain himself. Ha! ha! ha!

M. F: Manufactured it himself! Why, what do you mean!

Ful: I mean that he has invented a rainproducing machine, and this disturbance of the elements is merely a result of his showing me how the apparatus is manipulated.

M. F: What! a rainproducing machine!

Ful: Yes, a rainproducing machine. And ten chances to one the professor will be a very wealthy man, some day, just on account of that invention. Oh, Flat Carr has got a dead cinch on the soft water supply, all right; there's no doubt about that.

⟨Enter T. H., rear.⟩

T. H. ⟨Similtaneously.⟩ A-hum!

(Ful. looks up)

Ful: Well boys.

B. T. Excuse us, but all th' clocks hev struck, an' we can't bring 'em to time.

Ful: B-b-b-r-r-r! Well, this IS serious. What did they strike for?

B. T: Shorter hours and larger figures.

Ful: So, so! Let me think! ah, yes! well, here's the key to the situation (Hands Ben a large wooden key) Start the works and get some new hands. That will teach them to be more watchful in the future.

T. H: (Similtaneously.) Why, of course.   [Bow.]

Ful: Now, take these eggs and go out and set the clocks. (Hands each an egg.)

T. H: (Sim.) Why, of course.

(Bow, kisses at M, F., and exeunt, rear.)

Ful: (Sitting) Curious fellows those, — curious fellows; eh, Miss Fitt; But our conversation, my dear young lady, our conversation. We were speaking of Flat's rain producing machine, I believe; were we not?

Miss Fitt! Yes, and I am certain now that our inventive friend as you call him, is a much more intelligent man than I thought him to be when first I saw him.

Ful: Well, probably he is, probably he is —as far as inventions go; but I think that beyond mechanical contrivances he is seriously lacking, my dear young lady, seriously lacking.

M. F: I'm sure I don't see in what way, he seems to have positive genius in some lines, and he wouldn't be so very bad looking if he were fixed up.

Ful: But take for example, this matter of himself and Elizabeth Unit. Now, he doesn't seem to possess the nerve, the sand, so to speak, to work for his own interests in this matrimonial race; and as things now stand, to me it looks very much as though Otto Sight, his unscrupulous cousin, would yet snatch the prize before Carr himself even gets a sight of it. However, I have decided to help him out all I can, and I feel certain that if you, my dear young lady, will also proffer your aid, we can make the inventor's prospects of gaining a home and fortune very much brighter indeed. Now, Miss Fitt, will you join with me in this relief expedition?

M. F: Well, let me think over it for a moment. [In soliloquoy.] Perhaps it would be well to force Helena to bring this matter to a climax as soon as possible, so that I may judge by substantial evidence if Otto Sight really is as unscrupulous as he appears; so that I may see if he really would try to resort to force, as I overheard him threaten, And if he should turn out to be a villain, I can easily bring matters to a quick close by a full explanation. (To Ful.) Well, I have decided.

Ful: And your decision is?

M. F: That I am willing to do all in my power to help you.

Ful: Good, good, good! But what is to be done at all must be done at once, my dear young lady, and—

[Peculiar harsh noise from without. Enter Prof., L.]

Ful: (Rising.) What was that?

Prof: That was me, drawing my breath.

Ful: ‖Handing slate.‖ Well, here's your slate and pencil. Draw it for me, will you?   (Exit Prof., L.)

Ful: B-b-b-r-r-r! Now, we must get to work quickly, my dear Miss Fitt, lest the crafty Otto Sight should formulate some new plan, since his fishing party idea is made impracticable. But though there is no time to be lost, there is one thing we must not forget, and that is that the professor has not yet seen this Elizabeth Unit, and is under the impression that she is a very beautiful woman. Now, I HAVE seen her, and I know that should Lectric Carr once get a glimpse of her face before he has proposed the fatal question, he would have nothing more to do with the affair, whatever,—promise or no promise, fortune or no fortune.

M. F: Well, can't we do something to fix that? Can't we blindfold him, or——

Ful: The very idea! Just the thing! Excellent! That will make the way all clear before us, I think. [Rising.] But come; the time for action is here, and we must begin.

M. F: But what am I to do?

Ful: Well, all I require of you, my dear young lady, all I re-

quire of you is to bring Elizabeth Unit to this room, telling her
that Lectric Carr wishes an interview. Leave all else to me.

M. F: With pleasure. But you want to be careful, my boy,
that you don't get smitten with her yourself. The girl is a charm-
er.

Ful: What kind? A snake charmer?

M. F: Oh, my, no! A watch charm-er something of that sort.
You see, she charms people's watches till they can't move, as
soon as she turns her face on them. Well, tra-la-la! You'll suc-
ceed all right in making a match between her and Lectric Carr,—
I don't think!   [This last aside. Exit, rear.]

[Enter Prof., R.]

Prof: Well, sir. this is the dryest rain I ever saw. · I'm goin'
out and wet my whistle. (Moves L. Ful. comes down from
rear door.)

Ful: Say, professor.

Prof: Well, what can I do for me.

Ful: Yes.

Prof: Why, so do I. How did it happen?

Ful: Well, I'll tell you about it. Where have you been?

Prof: Well, I've just been up on the roof trying to tie a rain-
bow, but the rain was falling pretty fast, and I got a drop too much
So I thought I'd come down.

Ful: So, so! And did you get anything to eat?

Prof: Well, no. I looked for some eggs, but I couldn't find
any. I guess they must have been mislaid·

Ful: Eggs-actly! Eggs-actly! But I have good news for you,
professor.

Prof: Good news! What is it? Have the Brightsvillians re-
leased me from my promise?

Ful: Oh, no. But Miss Fitt and I have agreed to give you all
the assistance in our power to help you win the girl and the fortune.

Prof: Oh! Well, thank you, thank you. I'll be glad of your
assistance—— nit..

Ful: Yes; Miss Fitt said that you stand as much show and
even more than the other fellow.

Prof: Oh, yes. And was that all?   (Expectantly.)

Ful: No; she also said that you arn't half a bad fellow, and you
are really very brainy.

Prof: (Bowing.) Oh, thank you, thank you.

Ful: And she stated further that you might be a very good-
looking person if you had another face.

Prof: Oh, thank you, thank you. Do you know, I always did
admire that Miss Fitt from the moment I first saw her. She's a
mighty fine girl.

Ful: Yes? But we are wandering from our subject, my dear sir, we are wandering from our subject. Miss Fitt is at this moment on the errand of bringing Elizabeth Unit here to have an interview with you, and though I regret it greatly, I shall have to blindfold you, sir, I shall have to blindfold you! (Produces handkerchief.)

Prof: Blindfold me? I guess not! It cannot was. (Comes down.)

Ful: But it must be.

Prof: Must! I'd like to know why.

Ful: Well,—a—hum—that is, well, love is blind, you know, love is blind, and —

Prof: Well, this isn't a case of love.

Ful: But the lady is so extremely beautiful that I am afraid she will dazzle you if your sight is not obstructed. (Feminine voices from without.) There: they're coming now. Well, what do you say?

Prof: Oh this is so sudden: Well, all right, If she's beautiful, that settles it.   [Ful. blindfolds him.]

(Enter Miss Fitt and Elizabeth Unit.)

Ful: [Still tying.] Pew! what a close shave.

Prof: A close shave? Why, I haven't had a shave for a week. I tried to shave myself——

Ful: S-s-sh! They're here!

(Shakes hands with Eliz.)

Ful: Mr. Carr desires an interview with you, my dear Miss Unit You must not mind the bandage he wears. He once witnessed a preformance of the "BLACK CROOK" and has had sore eyes ever since.

Eliz: Poor fellow!

Ful: But allow me. Miss Unit; Mr. Carr; Mr. Carr, Miss Unit.

Prof: Happy to meet you.   (Bows in opp. d irection.)

Eliz: Won't you shake hands, professor.

Prof: Why, certainly.   ‖Gropes. Shakes.‖

[Prof, comes down with Ful.)

Prof: You ain't goin' to leave me alone with that' woman, are you?

Prof; Of course.

Prof: Well, I wish you'd stand around outside, and if he should get wild, don't let her hurt me?

Ful: Nonsense! Nonsense! But, Miss Fitt, we must be going, we really must.

M. F: Yes; let's see if we can find the girls.
          ‖Exeunt, rear.‖

Prof: Won't you be seated?

Eliz; Thank you.   (Both sit. Embarrassed.)
Prof: (Aside.) I wonder why she don't say something.
Eliz: ‖Also aside.‖ I wonder why he don't say something.
                    (Slight pause.)

Prof: ⎱
        ⎰ It's been a beautiful day.
Eliz: ⎰

                    (Slight pause. Confused.)

Prof; ⎱
        ⎰ Yes.
Eliz: ⎰

                    (More confused. Pause.)
Prof; (Opening a book, You've got a kind, good face.
Eliz: Thank you.
Prof: Don't mention it,   ‖Pause.‖
Eliz: ‖Aside.‖ Well, he may be a smart man, but he can't talk.
I'll have to say something. Professor, can you swim?
Prof: Swim! Well I should say yes.
Eliz: Why, where did you learn to swim, Professor?
Prof: In the water. I've been in the swim as long as I can re-
member.
Eliz: Well, that's doing pretty well for an old man.
Prof: An old man! Why, I'm not an old man. You ought to
see me when I'm dressed up. Why, I'll bet I'm no older than
you are. By the way, how old are you, anyhow?
Eliz: Oh, I'm only sweet sixteen. (Clock on wall rings off.)
Prof; [After both looking round.] It's a false alarm. It's all
right. But tell me, do you know for what reason my friends—I
sought this interview?
Eliz; Ye-e-e-s,
Prof; Well, then, let's talk business.
Eliz; Not so fast. First I want to know something about you.
Do you drink, Professor?
Prof: Drink! Drink! Woman, do you mean to insult me!
No; I never drink.
                    [Enter T. H., rear.]
Ben: Say, Professor, won't you come down and have your
usual daily cocktail with us?
‖Prof. aims invention at them. Latter exeunt.‖
Prof: Oh, Liz, Liz, whenever I gaze upon your beauteous
countenance, my heart thrills with such a curious sensation that
words cannot express it, my tootsy wootsy, wootsy tootsy.
‖Then Prof. lies back in chair with tongue hanging out.‖
Eliz: He! he! he! Is that on the square?
Prof: Well, I've got a square in the other room. I can take
you in and show you.
Eliz: Well, age before beauty, you know, professor,—you go

first.

Prof: But there are times when even age, as you please to call me, bows before beauty, my dear Queen Elizabeth.   (Bows.)

Eliz: Queen Elizabeth!

Prof: Yes, Elizabeth,— queen of my heart.

[Exeunt, L.]

(Enter Ful. and M. F., rear.)

Ful; (Looking about.) B-b-b-r-r-r! Well, I see that they have already sought quarters more secluded. They must be getting on finely by this time.

M. F: Yes, so they must.

[Angry voices without. Enter T. H., dragging Ot. He throws them off.]

Ful: B-b-b-r-r-r! Gents, I demand to know what is the meaning of this.

Ot: It's a downright outrage, that's what—

T.H. (Sim.) Shut up!

Ben: Well, I'll tell you how it is. Yew see we wuz strollin' 'raoun ther house fer a little exercise, w'en we happened to overhear a grass plot between this here skunk [Indicating Ot. an' Silver Bill, th' Toughest Man in Town.

Ot: That's a lie and I can—

T. H: (Sim.) Shut np!

How: That Otter Sight he said as how Flat Carr was hevin' a talk with Lizzie Unit now, an' he thought the perfessor wuz succeedin' better'n he had, so he wanted tew hev it stopped. Then they began plannin' haow ter do it.

Ot: Don't you believe a word these scoundrels are—

T. H: †Sim.† Shut up!

Hoop: It's true, every word on it. An' they finally decided that Otto Sight should go intew ther room where Flat an' th' gal was talkin' an tell th' professor thet a man outside wanted ter see im. Then after Flat went down, Silver Bill wuz ter entice 'im ter ther bank uv ther Hudson an' then knock 'im on ther head with a Populist club. He was only ter hit him hard enough ter lay 'im up fer two er three weeks, so Otto Sight could persuade Lizzie ter marry him by givin' her a face powder in her coffee We waited till the New York sport started up ter Flat's room an then we nabbed 'im.

T. H: †Sim.† That's the truth, the whole truth, and nothing but the truth.

(Otto shakes fist, tries to escape C., but T. H. recapture.)

Miss Fitt: Then my suspicions were correct, and Otto Sight really is a villain of the deepest dye. Now my course lies plain before me.

(Rumpus without. Quick music, soft and low.)

Ful: Otto Sight, you're a contemptible scoundrel, sir, a contemptible scoundrel, and if you were rightly dealt with, you should be thrown into jail, sir, thrown into jail. Yes, sir.

(Quick music, loud. Enter Prof. followed Eliz. Prof. presents a rather ripped-up-the-back, appearance, and carries the bandage from his eyes.)

‡ Prof: Well, boys, it's all over. I absolutely refuse to try to win that freak for a wife!

CURTAIN.

Three Hoboes: What! Remember that tailor bill. Would you break your promise?

Prof: Well, that face is enough to break glass and crockery, much less promises. And now, if you decide to drop this matter, and allow me to live on in peace, an old bachelor, I'll carry on my inventing the same as heretofore and live here at the Porter House; but on the other hand, if you insist, I'll move to New York to live and give Brightsville the cold shoulder. Now which'll you have shoulder, or Porter House?

CURTAIN.

Act III.

VESTIBULE OF THE MUGG MANSION ON THE BANKS OF THE
ST. JOHNS RIVER.—MORNING.

[At rise, chorus by Miss Fitt, Lotta Fellers, Adeline More,
Elizabeth Unit, and Cole Black.]

[After chorus, exit Cole, R.]

Lot: Oh, girls, I've got the loveliest new beau! You just
ought to see him!

M. F: Let me think! That makes just a dozen you've had in
the last month, dozen it?

Lot: Yes, it dozen. But really, this one is the nicest of all.
He's going to take Adeline and me out for a sail this morniug.
Won't you go along?

M. F: Well, what is it?—a bargain sale?

Lot: No.

M. F: Then I can't go. I've got too mnch time on my hands
now to go yachting on a beautiful morning like this.

Ad. and Lot: Oh, that's too bad!

Ad: Now, I really ought to write a few letters before we go,
but I can do that when we get back.

Ad. and Lot: Good bye, good bye!   (Exit, L.)

(During conversation, enter Cole, begins dusting and putting
things to rights.)

M. F: It doesn't hardly seem as though a mouth had passed
since we left Brightsville, does it?

Eliz: No, but still it is true. I wonder what has become of
Otto Sight. Our ruse was very successful and now you have
decided, I suppose which——

M. F: [Placing finger on lips.] S-s-sh! Don't breath a word
about that yet. Even mules have ears. But the professor promised me he'd come here on a visit, soon,and if he intends to get
here before the summer's out, he'd better hurry up.

Eliz: Why, havn't you heard?

M. F: Heard what? herd of cattle?

Eliz: This is no time for joking. The professor started on his
trip yesterday, and expected to arrive here this morning, but the
train he was on was wrecked and he was instantly crushed to
death and buried in the debris.

M. F: ‖Starting in great agitation.‖ What! Oh, heavens, how
terrible! (Great agitation. Then masters herself. and assumes a
lighter air.] Poor professor! Oh, well, I suppose the wreck
was too much train on his delicate constitution.

‖Yacht whistles without. Numerous and vigorous.‖

Eliz: Oh, there's that yacht whistle again. I guess the girls
just merely went out on a toot trom the way it sounds. ‖Rising.‖

Well I'll run down to the landing. Maybe I have yet time to catch the yacht and have a ride.

‖Exit rear.‖

‖Cole is vigorously plying a brush to the furniture.‖

Miss Fitt; ‖Turning.‖ Well, Cole, I see you're out for the dust.

Cole: Yes'm, Yes'm, I'se out fo' d' dust. Oh, yes, indeedy, I'se out fo' d' dust.

(Accidently knocks clock from table to floor)

M. F: What are you doing? Trying to kill time? Why, you don't know how to dust. Here give me that, (Reaches for brush) and I'll show you how it ought—‖Glances at brush.‖ Why, what a peculiar brush.

Cole: †Enthusiastically.† Yes, 'm, yes, 'm. Dat bresh has got a hist'ry, missy, dat bresh has, fo' suah.

Miss Fitt; A history?

Cole: Yes, ma'm. One day w'en mah great-great-gran'-pap was out onto d'plains in d' Fah West, he hed a bresh wif d' Indians Well, dis am d' same ole' bresh!

†Exit R . C.†

Miss Fitt: ‡After a pause.‡ Why, that sassy nigger. But O, I can't help thinking of the poor old professor. What a horrible death! And he wasn't half a bad fellow! †Draws a bill from bosom.† I guess I'll send Cole out for a copy of the "Morning Wall Paper," so I can read the particulars of the wreck.

‡Money in hand, she turns towards rear door, which is covered by curtains.‡

Miss Fitt: ‡Calling as if servant were behind curtain.‡ Come here, Cole.

‡Enter Prof. Lectric Carr.‡

Prof: ‡Fanning with hat.‡ I ain't Cole, I'm hot.

Miss Fitt; Heavens! You here, professor? I thought you were dead.

Prof; No, but my clothes are quite faded, and I'm going to dye tonight. So you thought I was dead?

Miss Fitt: That's what I was told.

Prof; Goin' to spend that to see if I was dead, were you?

Miss Fitt: Yes

Prof: ‡Brief silence. Then snatching bill and pocketing it.‡ Well, I AM dead.

Miss Fitt: But professor, how did you escape from the wreck unhurt.

Prof: Why, I didn't come on the railroad at all. I came on my latest invention, my air ship. Oh, I had a high time. But ‡Eagerly.‡ you don't seem very glad to see me?

Miss Fitt: ‡Sadly.‡ Yes, I'm glad to see you, but yesterday I lost a very near and dear tooth, and I feel very sad today.

Prof: Oh, lost a very near and dear tooth, did you? Feel sad today? I'm so sorry. Can I do anything for you?

Miss Fitt: Well, you might do something sad. I think it would do me good.

Prof: Do something sad? What'll I be?

Miss Fitt: Be a tramp.

Prof: Be a tramp? A sad tramp? All right. [Assuming a plaintive tone, advances with outstretched hand.] Please gimme something to eat, missus, please gimme something to eat. I've only had three square meals today. I'm tryin' to get home to my poor wife and children, so I won't have to work any more.

Miss Fitt: (Pityingly.) Why, you poor man! You must be half-starved. Here, take this pie. [Hands him pie.] I know it's good, for I baked it myself. [Drops pie in handing it. It falls with a dull, sickening thud. Prof. stares a moment, and then turns disgustedly.]

Prof: Oh, say, let's play something else. But really, you don't seem very glad to see me back. I don't believe you are glad to see me back, I know what I'll do. (Draws and examines revolver.) I'll go out and shoot myself.

‡Miss Fitt runs after him, crying,‡ "No, no, no!" He exits. Report outside immediately. Miss Fitt shrieks. Enter Prof., with a bottle of beer frothing over at top.‖

Prof: (Attitude.) Have one with me? (Pouring out a glassful to Miss Fitt.)

‖Miss Fitt in great surprise, sinks into a chair.‖ Oh, heavens, this is too much.

Prof: Well, you can leave what you don't want. But say Cinderella,

Miss Fitt: Please don't call me Cinderella.

Prof: All right, Cinders. I wish I knew what to do with my revolver.

Miss Fitt: Well, why don't you let it go off and have a good time! [Silence a moment.]

Prof: Isn't that funny! †Laughs.† But no, I can't do that. But I'll tell you what I can do. I'm as dry as a fish myself, and my revolver's empty, too, so we'll just take this bottle of—-ice water, and both go out and get loaded.

(Pauses. Exit on quick music.)

(Enter at same time, Cole Black.)

Cole: Dey's five gem'men down here fo' t' see yo', missy, an' dey say fo' me t' bring dis yar kyard in t' youse. ‡Extends card,‡

Miss Fitt: Five gentlemen to see me! There must be some mistake. That must be Lotta Fellers they want to see. I never have more than two visit me at one time.

Cole: I ast dat ar my ownse'f, but dey swar to d' Lawd de want fo't' see youse. Read whut it sez on d' kyard, missy.

Miss Fitt: Good idea! I'll raise your wages for that, ‖Reads.‖ "It is our turn. We are here on a Summer Outing. We are the people. We are the hot things, Signed, Fuller Tawk and the Village Crowd." What! the village crowd here on a summer outing? Why, show them immediately.

Cole: [Bowing out.] Yes, missy, I show 'em in, I show 'em in.

(Exit, R.)

Miss Fitt: I hope the girls will get back from their yachting trip soon. They and the Three Hoboes from Hoboken can enjoy themselves hugely.

(Tragedy music. Enter Prof.]

Prof: (Tragically.) I fear I am lost, lost! How, shall I tell me child! They are still in me feetsteps!

Miss Fitt: What? Your shoes?

Prof: [Laughingly.] Why, you awful thing. But to speak in earnest, Otto Sight is here in the town. I saw him myself not more than a minute ago.

Miss Fitt: (Reflectively.) Ho, ho! Otto Sight and the Village Crowd here at the same time! Maybe they're together. This means something. [To professor.] Whom did you see him with?

Prof: (Looking at her, strangely.) With my eyes, of course.

Miss Fitt: I mean, was he with anyone?

Prof: ‡Quickly.‡ No.

Miss Fitt: Well, find him again, and don't let the young cur out of your sight for an instant.

Prof: Cur-rect.

†Exit, L. C.†

Miss Fitt: And now for the boys of Brightsville.

‖Quick music. Enter the Village Crowd, Fuller Tawk, and Cole, who stations himself at door.‖

Miss Fitt: Why, my dear friends, I'm awfully glad to see you I was never so surprised in all my life. How are you, anyhow?

Village C: ‖Shout to the tune of "Over the Fence Is Out."‖ We're all alive and kicking!

Miss Fitt: ‡Recoiling.‡ Oh, that strain seems strangely familiar to me! †Recovering.† But you gentlemen must be quite tired out with your long journey on the railroad, What line might you have come on, anyhow?

Fuller Tawk: Well, we might have come on the fish line——

Herrmann: Or dot clothes line——

Ben Thayer: Or the telegraph line——

Howland Yell: Or on the tape line——

Hooper Up: Or on the line of battle ——
All: But we didn't.
Herrmann: No, ve game on dose ships dot pass in der night.
     (All this done very rapidly.)
Miss Fitt: (Aghast.) And these people live in the country!
But excuse me for keeping you waiting, gentlemen. You must
be quite fatigued and wish to get quickly to your rooms to rest.
Cole!
  Cole: §Advancing.§ Yes, missy.
Fuller Tawk: [Waving him back.] Hold on! Not yet!
B-b-b-r-r-r! First of all we wish to tell you of the latest and
most absorbingly interesting piece of news now extant. All
Brightsville is shaken to the very core, to the very core, my dear
young lady, by the sudden and absolute disappearance of Miss
Elizabeth Unit. The very day you and your maid left Brights-
ville she disappeared as completely as if the earth had opened
and swallowed her up. There is a large reward offered for any
information as to her whereabouts, but the strangest part of the
whole affair is that there is no one, absolutely no one, my dear
miss, who can furnish the least clue which would lead to her dis-
covery.
  §Enter Otto Sight, suddenly.§
  Otto Sight: That's a mistake!
  Herrmann: ‖Starting, as do all others.‖ You!
     (Enter Prof. Hides in nich in wall.)
Otto: Yes . And I repeat it, when you say that absolutely
no one can give the least information as to the whereabouts of
Elizabeth Unit, you mistake. There is someone who can give
that information. And that person is——myself! †Surprise
among the listeners.‡, The lady was spirited away by my audac-
ious cousin, Prof. Lectric Carr. And he even now has her hidden away, and is at this moment endeavoring to force her to
marry him, so that he may receive the fortune which rightfully
should belong to me.
  ⸢Prof: Hidden in r ich highly excited. Rolls up sleeves,
and at this cue, rushes out. Otto Sight sees him, and makes
quick exit, followed by Prof.‖
  Herrmann: †Looking all around.† Undt vere iss Oddo Sightd?
  Miss Fitt: He's out o' sight. I easily see through the fellow's
game. He's still hard at work trying to blast the professor's
reputation. And I hope none of you will believe a single word
of what he just said.
  Three Hoboes: Of course not.   †Exit Her. and Ful., rear.†
  Miss Fitt: (Looking out of doorway.) Now, I suppose you
are all acquainted with my young lady friends who were with me
at Brightsville. And as they are with me now, I want to give

you a piece of good advice. Cultivate them. They're nice girls, none better. And, besides, they're noted for their good nature and non-quarrelsomeness,——especially their non-quarrelsomeness. Here they are now.

†Enter the girls, squabbling among themselves.‡

Lotta: Now you know he said I was the prettiest!

Adeline: I don't know any such thing! I'm perfectly sure it was me he meant!

Helena: And I know positively it was neither of you two, but me alone he referred to.

Adeline: He didn't!.

Helena: He did!

Lotta: He didn't.

Miss Fitt: Girls!

‡The girls catch sight of the Three Hoboes.†

Lotta: Well, of all things!

Adeline: You dear boys. Natural as life!

Helena: Why, I'm awfully glad to see you.

Miss Fitt: Girls!

Helena: How are all the dear old jays down at Brightsville, anyhow?

Miss Fitt: Come here, girls.

Adeline: Why, tell us all about it. When did you get in?

Miss Fitt: †Impatiently.‡ Girls, do you hear me?

‡They turn. She takes them aside.‡

Miss Fitt: Those Three Hoboes from Hoboken are well heeled, girls, and if they happen to ask any of you to be their life partner or that they would like to have you help them in this hard battle of life, or any of that sort of chaff, it might be a good thing to take them up. A word to the wise——(Wink.)

‡Girls nod, and return to Three Hoboes.‡

Lotta: Eh,——wouldn't it be a good plan, don't you think dear boys, to go out and see the grounds, and the river, and the yachts, and all the beautiful things we have out here?

Ben Thayer: Well, I don't know but what it would be a good scheme. Don't you think so, boys?

Other Two: Why, of course,

Ben Thayer: Well, here goes, then!

(Lotta takes Ben's arm, Adeline Howland's, and Helena Hooper's.)

(Exeunt, laughing and talking.)

Enter Herrmann and Fuller Tawk.

Fuller: B-b-b-r-r-r! Lovely grounds you have here, my dear miss, lovely grounds you have here, and so extensive, too. Why, this last tramp, combined with our long railway journey, has really tired us completely, Herrmann and I. Cole, will you show us to our rooms? We are ready now.

Cole: Yes, sah; Yes, sah; right dis way, gem'men, right dis way. ‖Starts L.‖

Miss Fitt: ‖Pointing R.‖ The other way Cole. Give the girls a chance!   †Exeunt R.†

Miss Fitt: Ah! verily, the village person is a queer bird. He may be keen as a hawk, he may have the perception of an Eagle, but in spite of this, he will always be always a jay.

†Several shots without. Enter Prof. revolver in hand.†

Prof: ‡Excitedty.‡ Say, have you seen Otto Sight?

Miss Fitt: †Also excitedly.† Why,   no! What's the matter with him?

Prof: Well, there's nothing the matter with him yet. But I'm looking for him. Why, the idea of that man accusing me of abducting that old horror. I can see her terrible face now. B-b-r-r! away, away, awful vision, away! B-b-r-r! Ugh! Oh, if I only had Otto Sight here now! If he were only some place where I could reach him, I'd——

Voice from behind C. curtain: †Ben Thayer.† Now I've got a proposition to make you.

‖Prof: Astonished.‖

Voice: I'll come to the point right away. Will you be my partner for life?

Prof: Otto Sight and an associate!

Voice: Oh, relieve this suspense, and tell me, will you help me on in this great battle?

Prof: He's trying to persuade someone to help him blast my reputation!

Female Voice: ‡Lotta.† What great battle?

Prof: A woman!

Male Voice: This great battle of life.

Female: O, Ben, this is so sudden!

‡Volley of kisses. Prof. growing more and more excited, rushes, at this cue, and draws open curtains on C. door. There on a long bench sits the Three Hoboes from Hoboken, and the Up-To-Date Girls. Each of the Hoboes has great sploth of powder on coat.‡

CURTAIN

TABLEAU TWO.

MUGG MANSION'S VESTIBULE, ON THE ST. JOHN RIVER'S
BANKS.

‖At rise, enter Prof. and Ful, L‖

Ful: B-b-b-r-r-r! Professor, what do you thing of the strange disappearance of Miss Elizabeth Unit, sir, what do you think of this most extraordinary occurrance?

Prof: Well, to tell you the truth, I don't think anything about it, and I care a whole lot less. When it comes to marrying anything, I consider, as compared to her, a baboon as a great deal better thing.

Ful: Yes, and I understand you've got your eye on a great deal better thing.

Prof: Well it's not a baboon. No; I confess that I have formed quite an attachment, of late, for our friend Miss Fitt. I am quite undecided whether to ask her to have me or not. I've thought hard on the matter several times, but I forget now what I thought. There's only one thing left for me to do. I'll have to think it over.   §Exit C.‡

Ful: Why do I linger here in the land of flowers, when long e'er this I should have been back at work with my partners in the city? But the place is so delightful, the people so interesting, that I can hardly tear myself away. But the best of friends must part, and I fear I can not remain many days longer.

‖Enter Prof., L.‖

Prof: [Holding up a corn popper.] Well I've decided, I'm goin' to pop.

Ful: So! so! And when do you intend to broach the subject the buxom Miss Fitt?

Prof: Well, I don't know. Shall I go and find her right away and determine my fate at once? Oh, what's the use? No use! No: I'll wait awhile. and to steady my nerves, I'll get a glass of water and a stomach cake,——or something a little stronger.

Ful: Ahem! B-b-b-r-r-r! I think I am in need of a little stimulant myself, my dear sir, so I'll just go along with you.

†Exeunt R. C.†

‡Enter M. F. and Hel.‡

Hel: Yes. We girls are going to begin rehersals today for our grand lawn fete. It will be a magnificent affair, among the beautiful roses, and palms, and magnolias. Don't you think so, dear?

Miss Fitt: Undoubtedly, but my dear girl, look me straight in the eye.

Helena: Yes. ‡She does so‡

Miss Fitt: (Slowly and deliberately.) Now answer me truly. Why—did—you—tell— me—-that—Prof,—Lectric—Carr—had—been—killed—in—a—railroad—wreck?

Helena: †Laughing merrily.† Oh, that? Why, I just did that for a cod.

Miss Fitt: Well, I thought it sounded rather fishy.

§Closing bars of a song floats in through the door.§

Helena: There! The girls have begun rehearsing already. I must hurry. or I shall certainly be late. Olive oil!

Miss Fitt: I wonder if that malicious Otto Sight is still prowling about here. I'd like to give him a piece of my mind.

| Walks out of rear door and looks R and L.||

‡Enter Prof., R.‡

Prof: Well. I never was so thirsty before in all my life. There is nothing more to drink in the house but water. I don't see water man's going to do. Hello, there's a bunch of keys. ‡On table.‡ I'll look and see, maybe I can find a whis-key.

†M. F. advances.†

M. F: Hello, professor.

Prof: †Strangely||. Hello.

§Silence, M. F. sits.||

Miss Fitt: Anything the matter, professor?

(Prof. advances clumsily, falling over a potted plant).

Prof: Miss Fitt, I've got something of vital importance to say to you, and I'm not going to beat about the Anhauser-Bush. I—ah—somehow, the more I've seen of you, the more I like you, and—and—I want you to—(Whispers) Now, what do you say?

(Orchestra cue. Strain from "Do, dó, My Huckleberry Do.")

Prof: Tnat's good advice.

Miss Fitt: (Aside.] Well, I might do worse. I'll risk it. [To Prof.] Professor, I yield to your wishes, I'll be yourn.

Prof: Oh, thank you! thank you! thank you! You'll never regret it. You shall have horses and carriages, and cows and pigs and all your heart desires. You shall have——

(Enters T. H. talking——Prof. yet on knees, begins to busily tie Miss Fitt's shoestring.]

Prof: [Looking at her foot.] Are you from Chicago?

Ben: We came in to tell you that we're going down town to take in the sights.

Miss Fitt: Well you want to look out that you don't get taken in yourselves. A very tough crowd hangs out there, and if they once lay hands on you, they'll very likely rob you of every cent you have to your name, and do you up pretty badly besides. Many a man has been caught the same way.

Ben: Oh, you needn't worry about us. We're able to take care of ourselves. "Just Tell Them That You Saw Us."

(Exeunt T. H.. rear.)

Miss Fitt: Well, they're going out for a good time.

Prof: Yes and now that they're gone, won't you name the

happy day, when we shall be made one. Ws shall have a wedding banquet fit for the gallery-gods. When shall it be, next month or Christmas eve?

Miss Fitt: Neither. It shall be this very afternoon, as soon as we can get a minister.

Prof. What!

Miss Fitt: Now don't make any remonstrance, dear boy: I have a certain reason for this which I will divulge later. It's all right.

Prof: Oh. this is so sudden! But I don't care. The sooner the quicker. Let us away, away, and be united.

(Chorus and, exeunt.)

SPECIALTIES,

[After specialties, enter Prof. and Rev, G. C.]

Rev. G. C: Oh, such a lovely day, Mr. Carr, such a lovely day to be united in the holy bands of wedlock. Have you ever thought how the good Lord has looked after every little—
Say, I want that cash!

Prof: Cash! What cash!

Rev: Why my fee for marrying you.

Prof: Fee! Great heavens', I don't see what I'm going to do.

Rev: I'd like to know why not.

Prof: Why, I havn't got a cent myself and my wife lost her pocketbook with all her ready money in it, a few moments ago. The Three Hoboes are the only ones who have any money and they've gone down to the village to see the sights. The only possible thing we can do is to wait for them.

Rev: I do believe they're coming now. And I shall have my fee, then, after all.

(Orchestra cue, "Comrades, Comrades," Enter Three Hoboes, clothing tattered and turn—pockets insidv out.)

CURTAIN.

TABLEAU THREE.

SCENE, ON THE ST. JOHN RIVER'S BANKS. MORNING ROOM
OF THE MANSION OF THE MUGG'S,

(At rise: Miss Fitt and Three Hoboes—former standing—
latter sit)

Miss Fitt: The orange, gentlemen, is the typical fruit of this beautiful land. Growing amidst the laughing and dancing wild flowers, basking in the tropical warmth of the matchless Florida sun, forming a verdant resting place for the fluttering golden butterflies, it seems to embibe all the delightful sweetness of the balmy scented air, the dainty blossoms, the delicate magnolias, and the fragrant blushing roses. In its original living state on the tree, the orange may be faultfully likened to the Summer Girl of our more northern clime, for

It has leaves in great profusion,—that for finery she wears,
It has smoothness, O such smoothness—that's for speech,
It has sweetness overflowing,—shat's for manner, when with
                                        beau.
She gaily trips along the sandy beach.   [THIN,—
Its pulp is made much sweeter by a cov'ring TIGHT AND
The maid is made the same, when by the sea.
'Tis very soft, the orange;
Yes, 'tis soft as soft can be,—
And the Summer Girl.——

Don't mention it. Oh dear boys, there's nothing like it.

Hol: Well, that may be all very well, ez fur ez it goes, but in my mind peelin' a orange is er skin game. W'en it comes right down tew grub, I want suthin' more substantial.

Ben: [Piping up.] Yes, an' I wouldn't mind hevin' suthin' ter eat right now, seein' ez we hain't foddered since dinner time.

M. F: Why, that's so.   (Presses electric button.)

[Enter Cole, R.]

M. F: See that lunch is prepared immediately for these gentlemen, Cole.

Cole: (Starting off.) Yes. missy,

(Enter Prof. R.)

Prof; And say, Cole,

C: Yes. sah.

Prof: I'd like to have door jamh on my bread.

C: Yes, sah; a'right sah. Yo' want it spread on bofe sides, sah?

Prof: Well, yes, and you can take it up stairs in the sleeping room and make it a bed spread.

C: Yes, sah; a'right, sah.

Prof: And Cole.

C: Yes, sah.

Prof: Be sure to have two or three lamps at my place at the table. I always like a light meal.   (Exit Cole, L.)

Hoop; I hope that nigger gets a hustle on the lunch. I'm holler as a drum.

Prof: Well there's a bulldog out in the kitchen. If you're all so hungry, why don't you go out and get a bite?

(Silence. Then T. H. rise. Another pause.)

T. H: ‡Sim.‡ We will. Another pause. Exeunt rear.

M. F: Say, professor, have you heard the latest news?

Prof: No, what is it?

M. F: Why, father shot mother with a revolver yesterday morning and the bullet went clear through her head.

Prof: Well, she didn't mind a little thing like that, did she?

M. F: Oh, no. Why it went in one ear and out the other.

Prof: Yes, mother always was that way. ‡Consults book.† I see that electric lights are being used now in almost every part of the civilized world.

M. F: Is that so? Why, I had no idea they were becoming that common.

Prof: Oh, yes. Why, even the florist down town is going to put in a plant.

‡Enter T. H., R.‡

Howl: Excuse us, but a stray bonfire just wandered into the house without knocking. What'll we do about it?

M. F: What! a stray bonfire wandered into the house without knocking? Why, go put it out at once.

Prof: Yes, go put it out at once.

T. H: Why, of course.   ‖Exeunt R.‖

M. F: You know that Mrs. Ebbsmith, don't you professor?

Prof: Yes.

M. F: Well, she just bought an elegant diamond ring. Oh, it's a beauty.

Prof: Is that so? Why, she's notorious. It must be a chip diamond.

‡Enter T. H., R.‡

M. F: Well, what's the matter now?

Hoop: Why, when we tried to put out that bonfire it got hot in a minute, and the flames were going to lick us.

M. F: Well, you shouldn't mind a little thing like that. Go fire it right off.

Prof: Yes, go fire it right off.

T. H: Why of course.   ‡Exit to R.‡

†Prof. sits at table and falls asleep, Miss Fitt shakes him.†

M. F: Come, wake up.

Prof: §Sleeply.§ G'way.

M. F: Come, now, you can do that some other time.

Prof: Why, what's the matter with you! This jis s-leap year.
†Cuckoo clock on wall strikes.†

M. F: I tell you what it is, dear boy, that clock's a daisy,
isn't it?

Prof: Well, I should say yes. Why it's a cuckoo.

Miss Fittt You never saw a picture of me when I was young,
did you, Jakey?

Prof: No; I nefer hat dot bleasure, Rachael.

Miss Fitt: Well, you've been talking to me so much about
my beauty and your love and all that sort of thing, that I
thought you might want to see one. That picture is of me.
Pointing to picture on wall.‖

Prof: Oh, isn't it nice! I always liked those sweet, pretty in-
fantile little pictures. I suppose it's a constant reminder of the
days, many long, long, long, long years ago, when you were
young.

Miss Fitt: Yes, there isn't a day goes by, but what it comes
in handy. (Quick music—Enter Cole, carrying ladder. Places
ladder before picture, opens latter like a door. takes out two bot-
tles, shuts picture, picks up ladder. Exit R. Professor stands
and then exits after Cole.)

Miss Fitt: [Picking a pair of gloves from C table.] Hello! I
can't have this. I'll have to put these kids to bed. [Exit R.‡
§Enters Otto skulking.§

Otto: The coast seems to be clear for a moment. If I only
knew where the lawyer's room is, so I could find the will. He
has it locked in his valise,—but once I place my hands upon it,
he shall neer see it more. With the will destroyed, I can safely
claim the fortune as my own. Now to find the room .

Approaches L door, nearly reaches it when Ful. steps in reading a paper—stands still. Otto starts for rear door—T. H. step
through, reading paper, stand. Otto starts for L. C. door, Cole
steps through, reading paper, stand. Otto starts for R. door,
Her. steps through, reading paper, stand.‖

Ot: †At bay.† Well gentlemen! †Glances up.†

Her: Donnervetter nachemal! Otto Sightd, vot you doo
here ad dis dimes off der nacht, eh, don'dt id?

Otto: Why, I-er-that is-a-ahem-I-I came to see Prof. Carr.

Her: Vell you gan'dt see him now.

Otto: Why not? Is he dead?

Her: Vorse,—he's married.

Otto: What! Married! married? My God! And the woman
who was fool enough to marry him—who is she?

Her: Miss Fidt!

Otto: What! Miss Fitt! Is this really true? Why, when he told us at Brightsville that he wouldn't marry Elizabeth Unit on account of her homliness, I thought he was working a bluff on me and was up to some little game. However if he's married Miss Fitt in earnest, I've got the whole field before me, and can marry Elizabeth Unit myself and get the cash.

Her: By dot vay, speaking of Lissy Unit, no trace off her has efer yet peen found. You saidt dot der professor had shtole her vay, put so long as he's married soo Miss Fitt, he gand't haf her.

Otto: That's true, curse the luck! And if he has not got her, then where on earth is Elizabeth Unit? †Enter M. F., R. sudn'ly†

M. F: Right here, my child.   ‡Silence‡

Otto: You! No this must be a mistake. Why, you are Miss Fitt, herself!

Miss Fitt: Know then, that Miss Fitt and Elizabeth Unit are one and the same.   (Enter Prof., R. C.)

Prof: That's the truth. She told me about it herself not more than ten minutes ago.   (Exit Prof., R. C.)

Ot: These two are one and the same! Why, what do you mean?

M. F: Just this: When I recieved word of the death of my dear old friend, Earnest Mugg, and learned the conditions of his peculiar will, I immediately determined to hide my identity so as to discover which of the two persons named in the will was most worthy of my hand. I joined your party, Otto Sight, when you were going to Brightsville on the Summer Outing required in the will; and I induced my maid, Helena Bandbox, to disguise herself with a horrible old maid outfit I once used in an amateur play. A day after our party arrived at the Porter House, my maid arrived in her novel make up and was duly installed as Miss Elizabeth Unit. My scheme worked well, as none of the people there had ever seen her, and did not know what I looked like. So I sat out to watch and take my choice of the two men by their actions in relation to Elizabeth Unit. I passing under the fictitious name of Miss Fitt. How well my idea succeeded you already know. How I discovered one by one, the many little plots to take unfair advantage over the professor; how I induced Lectric Carr, while blindfolded to propose to my maid; how after many little incidents of the same kind, I |discovered your plot, Otto Sight, to really do the professor bodily injury; How Elizabeth Unit was made to disappear by my made resuming her natural character while I still retained my assumed one, after our departure, are all known facts of the first water. And at length I decided. sir, that of the two, Prof. Lectric Carr is much the better man, and that you are a scoundrel. Hence I have ac-

acepted his offer, and am all ready his wife.

Otto: And—and this is true?

Miss Fitt: As gospel.

Otto: Well, then I guess my cake is dough.

‡Enters Professor, R C‡

Prof: Yes, and I've got the dough.

Otto: Curse the luck! ‖Whiningly.‖ But I ougut not to expect anything else. It has always been this way with me. Luck has always been against me as long as I can remember. There is only one way to change it. I will take my own life. [Snatches knife from relic on wall.] Lectric Carr. you have beaten me. You always was a deadbeat. Farewell! †Poises knife.†

Prof: Hold! the pen is mighter than the sword. I'm afraid your hard breast might break the sword. [Hands him pen.]

Otto: Bah! You talk as though I was the worst man on earth.

M. F: Well, you ought to have been behind the bars long ago. (Those holding newspaper. shake them.)

Her: Py de vay, shpeaking py pot, I haf readt, in dese baber dot you Otto Sight, are wanted in Seattle for bigamy, und you haf two vifes in udder barts off der gountry. ‡To others.‡ Vot shall ve doo abowt dot! Holt him, undt gif him oop soo de-offitcers!

⌐Otto tries to escape—T. H. hold him‖

Prof: Shall we? Oh, what's the use? No use! He can't do us any more harm, so we may as well let him go.

M. F: Perfectly correct. Otto Sight, we have nothing more to say to you. There is the door.   ‡Exit Otto, rear.‡

Howl: And now that we got rid of that scoundrel, I—we— (Indicating T. H.) would like a little piece of advice. You see we—that is—well we've got a little money saved up and—and—

‖Enter Up-To-Date-Girls‖

The Girls: (Eagerly.) Yes,—and—

Prof: ⌐Dramatically.‖ Ha! Villians, I understand. You wish to rob these innocent girls of their names. Have you not heard base scoundrels, that the only thing a girl has in this world is her good name. But it's a good thing.

M. F: Yes, go get married, and be happy—nit.

Prof: And I must give you something as a gift. ‡Draws out a huge wooden ring.——†Brokenly.‡ This is the same ring my poor old mother used to wear, when we were boys together. Here, divide it up among you. Bless you my children, bless you.

‡Enters Cole, breathlessly, rear.‡

Cole: ‡Excitedly.‡ 'Scuse me, sah, 'scuse me, but Otto Sight done climbed in to you aiah ship, and flew up 'bout fo' miles. An now he's stopped up dah, sah, an' he kaint go no higher, no come down, one way or anuddah. He's stuck in mid-aiah, sah, way up, 'bout fo' mile.

Prof: Well, that's a good place to leave him.

M F: Yes, he's as near heaven now as he'll ever be.

Prof: And now that everything has ended happily, will you all my friends, join my wife and I in a moonlight ride down the St. John river?

All: S-U-R-E, sure, sure!

Ensemble Specialty.

(Curtains over rear door drawn back, revealing moonlight scene, with the steam launch, "Elizabeth Unit," riding quietly at anchor.

CURTAIN.